# Daniel's Dog

By Jo Ellen Bogart

Illustrated by Janet Wilson

SCHOLASTIC
HARDCOVER

SCHOLASTIC INC./New York

To Mike D. and his ghost dog
J.E.B.


To my sons, Cory and Graeme, and the invisible bull dog, Bubba,
with special thanks to Cali
J.W.

Library of Congress Cataloging-in-Publication Data

Bogart, Jo Ellen.
    Daniel's Dog / by Jo Ellen Bogart; illustrated by Janet Wilson.
        p. cm.
    Summary: A young Black boy adjusts to the arrival of his new baby sister with the help of his
        imaginary dog Lucy.
    ISBN 0-590-43402-0
        [1. Imaginary playmates—Fiction. 2. Dogs—Fiction. 3. Babies—Fiction. 4. Brothers and
        sisters—Fiction. 5. Afro-Americans—Fiction.] I. Wilson, Janet, ill. II. Title.
    PZ7.B635786Dan 1989
    [E]—dc20                                                                        89-35258
                                                                                        CIP
                                                                                        AC

12  11  10  9  8  7  6  5  4  3          0  1  2  3  4  5/9

Printed in the U.S.A.                36
First Scholastic printing, March 1990

Daniel had a new baby sister named Carrie.

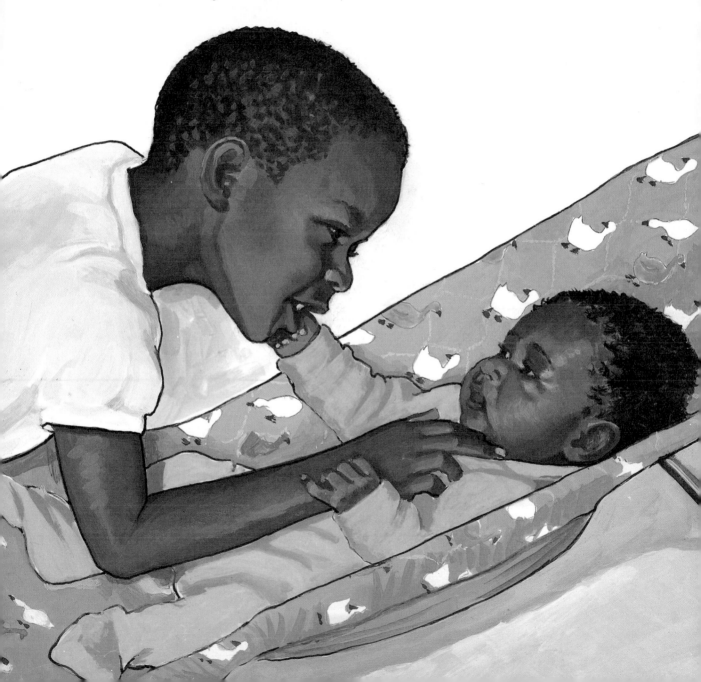

She had a tiny face and tiny hands. She couldn't throw a ball or play catch. She couldn't even talk. Carrie spent a lot of time lying on her back kicking her legs and a lot of time sleeping. Daniel's mother spent a lot of time taking care of Carrie.

Daniel could take care of himself. He made pillow forts on the sofa and ran his trucks on the rug. He rode his tricycle and shouted, "Rrhuum! Rrhuum!"

Sometimes he molded dragons out of play-dough. The dragons had big teeth and very long tails. Sometimes Daniel felt like a dragon himself. Then he would breathe fire, and roar and kick the pillows.

"Are you feeling mad at me, Daniel?" his mother asked one night as she tucked him in. "I'm sorry I haven't been spending as much time with you lately. Things will get better soon."

"I'm all right," Daniel told her, and smiled a little. "I'm just fine since Lucy came."

"Who is Lucy?" his mother asked.

"Lucy is my dog," Daniel explained. "My ghost dog. She always has time for me, no matter what."

"Oh, I see," Daniel's mother said. "Is she here now?"

"Right here next to my feet. She's nice and warm, and she likes it when I read stories to her."

Daniel's mother kissed him on his forehead. "Tomorrow will you read to me and Carrie?"

"Sure I will. Goodnight, Mom."

The next afternoon Daniel's friend Norman came over to play.

"Be careful," Daniel said, as Norman flopped onto the sofa. "Don't sit on my dog, Lucy."

"I don't see any dog," Norman said.

"You don't see her because she's a ghost dog. My grandpa sent her to me."

"But your grandpa died, Daniel. I remember — it was last summer."

"Of course he died," Daniel said. "How else could he be in heaven where ghost dogs live?"

"Really?" Norman's eyes opened very wide.

"Sure, Lucy was his ghost dog when he was little. He told me all about her. She came to him whenever he needed her, and now he's sent her to live with me."

"You're lucky, Daniel."

"I know, Norman."

Daniel's mother called from the kitchen, "Daniel, will you check Carrie for me? I think she's waking up and my hands are a greasy mess."

"Okay, Mom. Then Norman and I will take Lucy out to play. Dogs need a lot of exercise, you know."

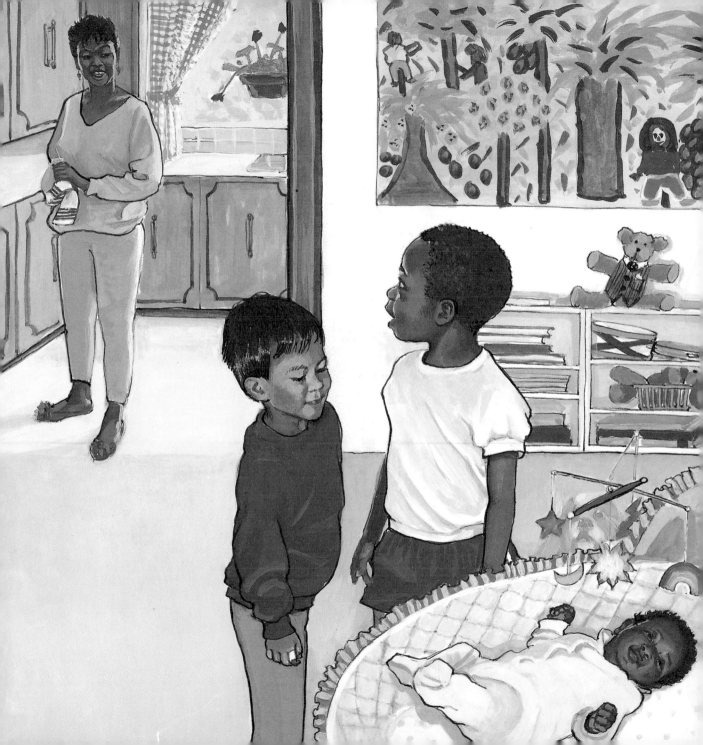

Daniel sang a song for Carrie while his mother washed her hands. Then he brought a diaper from the pile of clean ones on his mother's bed. His mother kissed him and said, "Daniel, you're a wonderful help to your sister and me."

Later, when Daniel's mother was feeding Carrie on the sofa, Daniel brought a book over. He couldn't read all the words yet, but he was very good at telling the pictures. "I picked an easy one," he told his mother, "because Carrie is just a baby."

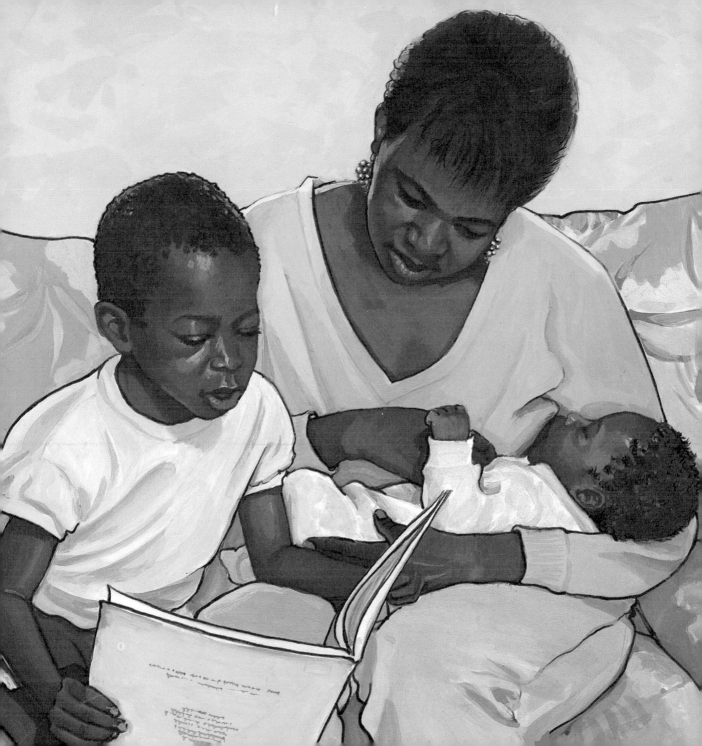

When Carrie was finished eating and had made a big burp, Daniel's mother asked him, "Would you like to hold her now?"

He nodded and made a cradle just the way she had taught him. His mother laid Carrie gently in Daniel's arms. He could feel how heavy she was. Carrie waved her arms around and one tiny hand hit Daniel's nose. Daniel laughed. Holding her felt nice.

"Where's Lucy?" Daniel's mother asked.

"She's here. She knows that I'm busy," said Daniel. "She understands that I'll play with her in a little while," he added.

When Norman came to play the next day, Daniel got out some paper and crayons. "Let's draw dinosaurs and alligators and swamp trees, Norman. You want to?"

Norman said yes, but he looked like he didn't really care. He looked sad. He was peeling little bits of paper off the green crayon.

"What's wrong, Norman?" Daniel asked.

"My dad has to take a trip for his work," he said. "I'm going to miss him a lot." Norman had tears in his eyes.

"I know what you need," said Daniel. "You need someone to keep you company while your dad's away."

"Who?" asked Norman.

"You need someone to sleep on your feet at night and listen to you read stories."

"Who?" Norman asked again, sniffling back his tears.

"Lucy has a friend named Max," Daniel said. "He's shaggy and grey and lots of fun. He could stay with you."

"I'd like that, Daniel," Norman said. "I'd take very good care of him, and he could come here with me to play."

"Lucy is smiling, Norman," Daniel said, "and wagging her tail."

"Yes," said Norman, "I can see that." He was smiling too.

Daniel picked up a crayon. "Lucy says Max will come to you at bedtime tonight. And she says this dinosaur needs some brown spots on top of the green."